To Mr. Lou
for finding me in the rubble

To Elena & Alessandra
for helping me to grow

Balzer + Bray is an imprint of HarperCollins Publishers.

The Digger and the Flower
Copyright © 2018 by Joseph Kuefler
All rights reserved. Manufactured in China.
No part of this book may be used or reproduced in any manner whatsoever without
written permission except in the case of brief quotations embodied in critical articles
and reviews. For information address HarperCollins Children's Books, a division of
HarperCollins Publishers, 195 Broadway, New York, NY 10007.
www.harpercollinschildrens.com

ISBN 978-0-06-242433-4

Typography by Joseph Kuefler
17 18 19 20 21 SCP 10 9 8 7 6 5 4 3 2 1
❖
First Edition

THE
DIGGER
AND THE
FLOWER

JOSEPH KUEFLER

BALZER + BRAY
An Imprint of HarperCollins Publishers

It was morning and the big trucks
were ready to work.

"Let's hoist," said Crane.

"Let's push," said Dozer.

"Let's dig," said Digger.

Together they built tall buildings for working.

They built roads for driving

and bridges for crossing.

They built and built until
the loud whistle blew.

"I'm beat," said Crane.
"Me too," said Dozer.

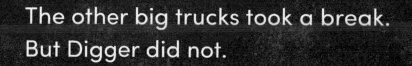

The other big trucks took a break.
But Digger did not.

He had found something in the rubble.

"Hello there," he said.
The flower was tiny, but it was beautiful.

Every day, while the other big trucks built,
Digger visited the flower.

He watered it when its leaves looked dry.

He shielded it on windy days.

And just before he switched off for the night,
Digger sang the flower a bedtime song.

BEV'S

The flower grew.
But the city grew, too.
Soon, every space had
been filled.

Every space but one.

"We need to put a building here," said Crane.
Dozer started his engine.

Before Digger could stop him . . .

Dozer blew a big puff of smoke

and cut the flower down.

Then the other big trucks went back
to work. But Digger did not.

When the smoke cleared, Digger
saw something in the rubble.

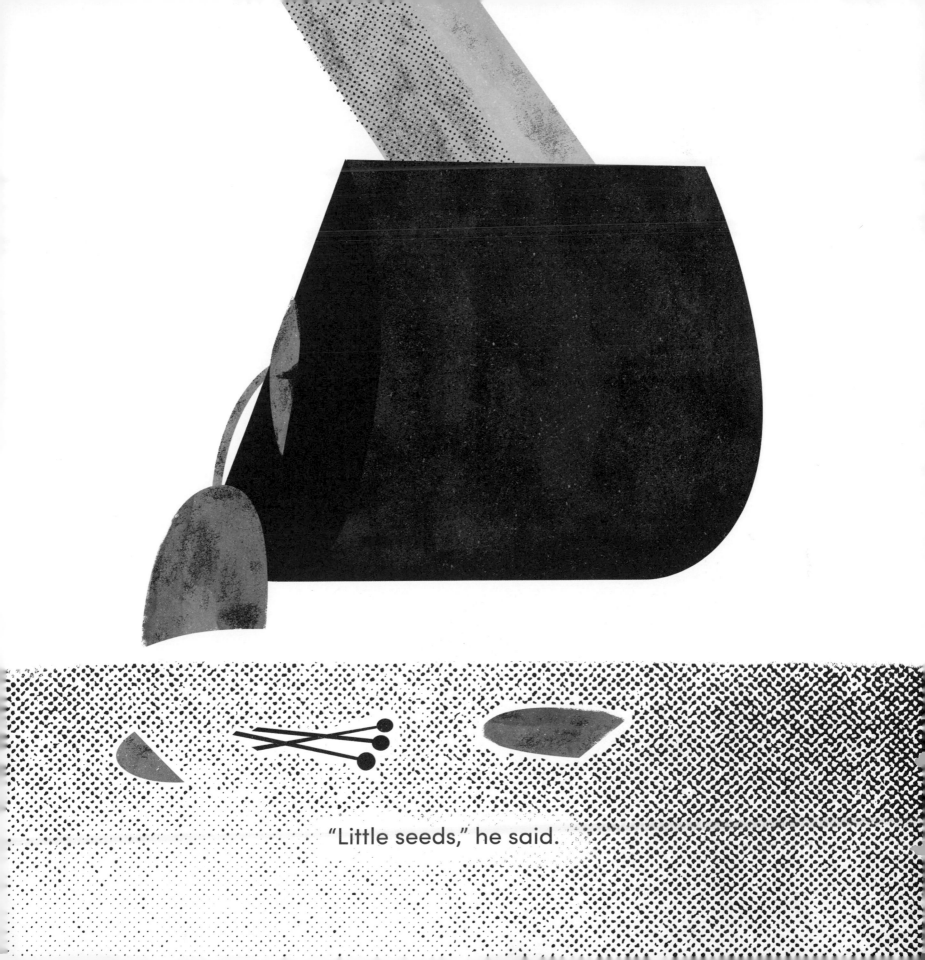

"Little seeds," he said.

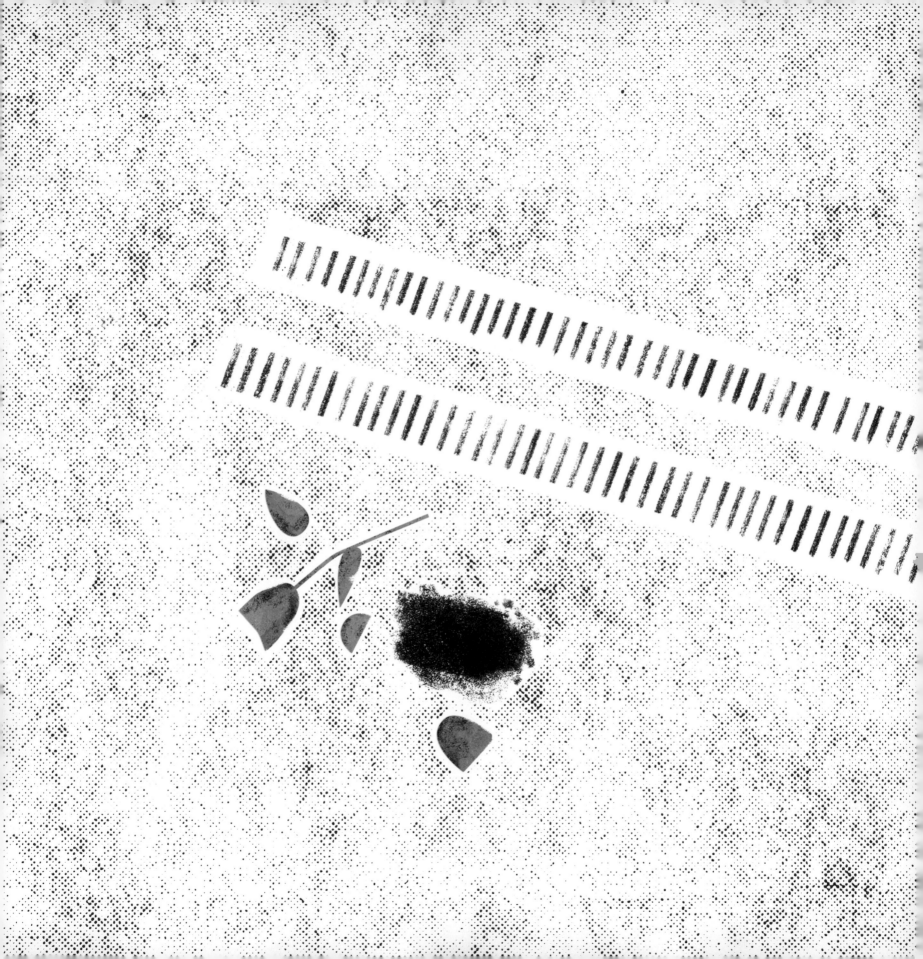

He scooped them up and drove.

He drove past the tall buildings.

Past the farthest house on the farthest street.

He drove to a place no big truck had ever been.

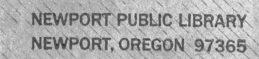

There, Digger stopped.
He dug and scooped . . .

and tucked the seeds
into the warm earth.

Every day, Digger cared for the seeds.
He watered them when their leaves looked dry.

He shielded them on windy days.

And just before he switched off for the night,
Digger sang the flowers a bedtime song.